U0098848

This book belongs to :

We Won the Lottery

We Won the Lottery

© 1996 Shoo Rayner

ISBN 0713645636

First published in 1996

by A & C Black (Publishers) Ltd., England

我家中樂透

Shoo Rayner 著／繪

刊欣媒體營造工作室 譯

三民書局

CHAPTER ONE
The Dreaming

$\mathcal{H}$ave you ever **dreamed** of **winning** the **Lottery**? Of course you have. I used to do it all the time.

第一章　夢想

　　你有沒有夢想過中樂透彩券的大獎呢？一定有吧，我就常常在想著這件事哦！

　　可以蓋一間好大好大的房子

　　沒有人會趕我上床睡覺

　　有私人專屬迪斯可，有很炫的燈光

　　有汽車

　　有超大瓦數的ＣＤ音響

　　沒有討厭的姊姊

　　還有……

　　還有……

　　還有……

　　也沒有姊姊臉上的雀斑

dream [drim] 動 夢想

win [wɪn] 動 贏得

lottery [`lɑtərɪ] 名 彩券

private [`praɪvɪt] 形 私人的

horrid [`hɔrɪd] 形 討厭的

Everyone in my family dreamed of winning the Lottery.

Dad wanted a new car.

My horrid sister, Clarissa, wanted Dig-Dig the **pop** star, that is. He's all she ever used to talk about.

我家裡的每一個人都夢想著能中樂透。

爸爸想要一部新車。

我那個惹人厭的姊姊——克萊里莎，則希望能見到搖滾明星狄格。她一天到晚把他掛在嘴上。

迪格！

如果我中了樂透獎，我就可以辦一場我的私人演唱會。

pop [pɑp] 名 流行樂

concert [`kɑnsɝt] 名 音樂會

As for my mum, she wanted to meet the Queen and have everyone call her Lady Jackson-Jones.

More than anything my mum wanted people to think she was really **posh**.

至於我老媽，她希望能見到女王，還要大家都尊稱她一聲傑克森─瓊斯爵士夫人。

其實呀，我媽媽是希望每一個人都覺得她非常的雍容華貴。

女王陛下

如果我們家中了樂透獎，那就比一些公爵還有伯爵夫人都還要有錢了。

as for... 至於⋯

posh [pɑʃ] 形 一流的；奢侈的

majesty [ˋmædʒəstɪ] 名 陛下

lord [lɔrd] 名 《英》貴族 (the Lords)

lady [ˋledɪ] 名 爵士夫人 (Lady)

Mum tries so hard. She only buys **tasteful** things in our town, then she goes **all the way** to the next town **(in the hope that** no one will **recognize** her), to buy the embarrassing stuff like spot-cream, toilet paper and... Lottery tickets. She thinks that really posh people don't do the Lottery, so we try to keep it a big secret.

Mum's so **stuck-up**, that when she married Dad, she put her maiden name in front of his.

Jones is frightfully common. Jackson-Jones is so much better. It's double-barrelled, don't you know?

That makes me John, Jarvis, Jackson-Jones! At school they call me J-J-J-John. It's a shame you can't choose your parents.

為了面子，老媽可是絞盡腦汁。在我們這個城裡，她只買高雅有品味的東西。然後，她會大老遠的跑到隔壁城裡（期望著不要碰到認識的人），去買會令她難為情的東西，像是有瑕疵的鮮奶油、衛生紙和……樂透彩券。她認為真正高尚的人家是不會玩樂透的，所以我們都把這件事當作是最高機密。

　　正因為媽媽是如此的愛面子，所以當她嫁給父親之後，還將娘家的姓氏擺在夫家姓氏的前面呢。

　　瓊斯這個姓太普通了，傑克森─瓊斯就好太多了。你知不知道這樣就成了複姓？

　　結果我的名字變成約翰‧加維斯‧傑克森─瓊斯(John Javis Jackson-Jones)！學校同學都叫我約─約─約─約翰(J-J-J-John)。不能選擇自己的父母親真是遺憾。

tasteful [`testfəl] 形 品味高雅的
all the way 千里迢迢地
in the hope that... 希望…
recognize [`rɛkəg͵naɪz] 動 知道；認出
stuck-up [`stʌk`ʌp] 形 自命不凡的

My friend Kevin likes to **wind** Mum **up**. If he stays at our house for tea, he always covers his food in tomato ketchup and asks where the chips are. Mum hates it!

Mrs Jackson-Jones? This spaghetti has got leaves in it.

Tee-hee!

Those are herbs, Kevin. Don't you know anything?

Clarissa, my horrid sister, really really **spoils** Mum's **attempts** to be posh. Ever since she fell in love with Dig, she's been wearing strange clothes and has stopped brushing her hair completely.

My daughter??? Goodness, no! We're just looking after her for a friend.

我的朋友凱文，愛讓我老媽精神緊張。每次他來我們家玩的時候，總是在整盤食物上倒上滿滿的番茄醬，然後再問說：「咦！洋芋片都到那兒去了？」媽媽非常討厭他這個樣子。

　　傑克森‧瓊斯太太，這個通心麵上面怎麼有葉子呢？

　　嘻嘻！

　　凱文，那個叫做香料，你懂不懂呀？

　　我那個討人厭的姊姊，克萊里莎，在她迷上了狄格以後，著實的打擊了我那愛慕虛榮的媽媽。因為她開始穿著一些奇裝異服，而且從此就再也沒有梳過頭髮了。

　　那不是我女兒！絕對不是！我只是替一個朋友照顧她而已。

wind [waɪnd] 勔 吊起；纏繞

wind...up 使…緊張

spoil [spɔɪl] 勔 破壞

attempt [ə`tɛmpt] 名 企圖

look after... 照顧…

CHAPTER TWO
Saturday Night

On Saturday nights we don't **actually** watch the Lottery but somehow the television always **happens** to be on.

Mum **pretends** to be writing out dinner party **invitations**, Dad pretends to be reading the paper, Clarissa pretends to be listening to her **Walkman** and I pretend to be doing my homework.

第二章　週末夜

　　在星期六的晚上我們不會特地去注意樂透的開獎，只是剛好那時家裡的電視都是開著的。

　　媽媽會假裝在寫晚宴的請帖，爸爸會假裝在看報紙，克萊里莎會裝作在聽隨身聽，而我呢，就假裝在寫家庭作業。

actually [`æktʃʊəlɪ] 副 確實；實際上

happen [`hæpən] 動 碰巧

pretend [prɪ`tɛnd] 動 假裝

invitation [ˌɪnvə`teʃən] 名 請帖

walkman [`wɔkmən] 名 隨身聽

On our big night, the Lottery program started **as usual. A couple of** winners got their checks, a brass band played a tune and received a lot of money to buy new **instruments**, and a tiny village in Scotland was given money to build a new sports hall. Then it was time to **concentrate** on this week's numbers.

Welcome, it's a roll-over week and tonight's jackpot is estimated to be over twenty million pounds.

在那個重要的夜晚，樂透開獎的電視轉播一如往常。有兩三個得獎者在領取他們的獎金，銅管樂隊一邊演奏一邊收下大筆的獎金，他們說要用這筆錢買新的樂器；蘇格蘭的一個小村莊得到了獎金，要蓋一座新的運動館。接下來，所有的人就集中精神在本週開獎的號碼上了。

　　大家好，這是樂翻天的一週，因為今晚的獎金估計至少有兩千萬英鎊。

usual [`juʒʊəl] 形 平常的

as usual 照常

a couple of... 兩三個的，數個的 （=a few, several）

instrument [`ɪnstrəmənt] 名 樂器

concentrate [`kɑnsn̩ˌtret] 動 全神貫注 《on》

jackpot [`dʒækˌpɑt] 名 獎金

estimate [`ɛstəˌmet] 動 估計

Mystic Maggie **appeared**, all dressed in black with moons and stars in her hair. She began making her **predictions**.

這時神祕的瑪姬出現了，一身的黑色，頭髮上掛著星星和月亮。她開始預言今晚的得獎者。

有一個得獎者是天蠍座的人。

就是我！

我看到一個正在看報紙的男人。

就是我！

我又看到一間紅色磚瓦的房子。

就是我們家呀！

一扇黃色的門而且上頭有一個數字１０。

就是我們！

我又看到了一個穿著有粉紅滾邊汗衫的人。

哦哦！

mystic [`mɪstɪk] 形 神祕的

appear [ə`pɪr] 動 出現

prediction [prɪ`dɪkʃən] 名 預測

Scorpio [`skɔrpɪ,o] 名 天蠍座出生的人；天蠍座

I turned bright red.

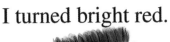

That's me!

Slowly...very slowly,
I lifted up my jumper.

I couldn't find a clean vest
this morning, so I borrowed one
of Clarissa's.

我的臉紅了起來。

是……是我啦！

慢慢地，慢慢地，我把毛衣掀了起來。

今天早上我找不到一件乾淨的汗衫，所以就向克萊里莎借一
件來穿。

I'd never really believed in Mystic Maggie's predictions before, but this was **uncanny**. We were really **excited**, and **for once**, we stopped pretending we weren't watching the program and gave it our full **attention**.

An old **comedian** I'd never heard of came on and told a few jokes...

...then he pressed the button to set the balls rolling.

我從來就沒有相信過神秘瑪姬的預言，但是這回真是非常不可思議。我們都興奮極了，所以就破例不再裝模作樣，開始全神貫注地看著電視。

　　一個我從沒聽過的老喜劇演員上臺說了一堆笑話。

　　是的，沒錯，我渾身充滿了銅臭味，因為……我已經一年沒洗澡了！

　　如果我今晚能中樂透，我將和你們分享。「樂」給你們，「透」就給我了！

　　我不介意增加點重量，我想增加個兩千萬磅（鎊）會讓我看起來更帥！

　　……接著他按下按鈕，彩球開始滾動了起來。

uncanny [ʌn`kænɪ] 形 不可思議的
excited [ɪk`saɪtɪd] 形 興奮的
for once 僅此一次 (=just for this once)
attention [ə`tɛnʃən] 名 注意力；注意
comedian [kə`midɪən] 名 喜劇演員
extra [`ɛkstrə] 形 額外的

We knew our numbers off **by heart**. They were all **based** on our birthdays.

The machine made its first **choice**.

Yes. Dad's age

Yes. Mum's age (she says)

Yes! My Birthday We'd won £10

Yes! Clarissa's Birthday

Yes! Dad's Birthday

Yes! Mum's Birthday!!!!!

我們早就背下那些號碼，因為都和我們的生日有關。

第一顆球開始掉出來了。

4 5　爸爸的年紀

3 0　媽媽的年齡（她自己說的）

5　　我的生日，我們曾經靠這個贏了 1 0 鎊

1 3　克萊里莎的生日

1 8　爸爸的生日

1 6　媽媽的生日

by heart 背下

base [bes] 勔 以⋯為基礎 《on》

choice [tʃɔɪs] 名 選擇

BINGO by JINGO!

WE'D WON!

We'd won the Lottery!

We didn't need to **bother** about the **bonus** ball.

WE'D WON THE LOTTERY!

「賓果！」

「中了！」

「我們中了樂透獎了！」

我們再不用關心特別獎。

「我們中樂透獎了！」

bother [`baðɚ] 動 煩惱

bonus [`bonəs] 名 紅利；獎金

*W*hat do you do when you've won the Lottery? When you've danced and sung songs and **hugged** each other all you can? When you've even hugged your horrid sister? Yuk!

How do you actually get the money?

Dad looked at the ticket.

Look, there's a phone number on the back.

第三章 中獎了！

　　當你真的中了樂透獎的時候會做什麼事呢？是不是高興的手舞足蹈，哼起歌來，還彼此緊緊相擁在一起呢？甚至還擁抱了那個討人厭的姊姊？中獎真好！

　　我們中了！

　　好吧，好吧……

　　萬歲！

　　我們中了！

　　真正的獎金會有多少呢？

　　爸爸看了彩券。

　　你們看！彩券的背面有電話號碼。

hug [hʌg] 動 緊緊擁抱

Mum phoned the number.

Yes... Yes... Yes... Yes...

They think that we're the only winner! They'll send someone round on Monday to confirm. They say we shouldn't tell anyone in the meantime.

But it was hard to keep quiet about winning the Lottery. Dad happened to **mention** it to his brother.

We...

...won...

And Clarissa happened to mention it to a friend that phoned.

媽媽打了這個電話。

是的。是的。

對。對。

沒錯！

好。好。好。

他們說我們可能是唯一的得獎者。星期一會派一個人過來我們家確認。而且啊！他們說這件事最好先不要跟其他人提起。

可是中了樂透獎這種事是很難守口如瓶的。爸爸湊巧和叔叔提起了。

克萊里莎則是跟打電話來的朋友提了一下。

confirm [kən`fɝm] 動 確認

mention [`mɛnʃən] 動 提到

And Mum thought she could trust her best friend.

...the...

...Lottery!

And I might just have mentioned it to my friend Kevin.

It was a big mistake.

I never knew we had so many friends and **relations**. By Sunday afternoon they were all in our sitting-room.

Need any help with your homework?

Hmmm.

We just happened to be passing!

媽媽覺得可以信任自己最好的朋友。

至於我，我可能只是跟凱文提了一下！

這些事真是錯誤到了極點。

在星期天的下午，他們全都坐在我家客廳裡面，我從來不知道原來我們家有這麼多親戚朋友。

要不要我教你作功課啊？

嗯……

我們剛好經過這附近！

relation [rɪˋleʃən] 名 親戚

No one actually mentioned the Lottery, but they all had the same **greedy** look in their eyes.

Eventually Dad had the **brilliant** idea of telling them we'd only got four numbers correct. They soon **disappeared**.

沒有任何一個人提到有關樂透彩券的事情，但是每個人都一樣貪婪地看著我們。

　　因為很久沒見到你們了，就過來拜訪一下。

　　嗨！

　　我給你帶來那本你要借的書。

　　四年前你借我的那支扳手我帶來還你了，真好用呀。

　　幸虧爸爸急中生智，告訴他們說我們只中了四個號碼。很快的，所有的人都走了。

greedy [`gridɪ] 形 貪婪的

eventually [ɪ`vɛntʃʊəlɪ] 副 最後，結果
　(=in the end)

brilliant [`brɪljənt] 形 頭腦機敏的

disappear [ˌdɪsə`pɪr] 動 消失

On Monday morning a lady from the Lottery came to see us. She looked very **stern**.

Hello, I'm Lolly Priceworth from the Lottery. I'd like to check the details on your ticket please.

She **noted** down the numbers and asked Mum where she'd bought the ticket. Then she went out to her car and made a call on her **mobile** phone.

第四章 通知

　　星期一早上，樂透公司的一位女士來到我們家，看起來非常的嚴肅。

　　你們好，我是樂透公司派來的蘿莉·普萊斯渥斯。我是來做確認工作的。

　　她抄下上面的號碼並且問了媽媽彩券是在那裡買的。接著便走進她的車子用汽車電話打了一通電話。

stern [stɝn] 形 嚴格的
detail [ˋditel] 名 細節
note [not] 動 記下 《down》
mobile [ˋmobl̩] 形 可移動的

When she came back her **frown** had gone
and her face had **split** into a huge smile.

當她再度出現的時候，原本緊繃的表情不見了，取而代之的是滿臉的笑意。

我很高興的在此向你們宣佈，你們總共……總共……總共……

多少？

多少？

到底有多少？

你們的獎金是……

是……

等等，我用寫的好了。

frown [fraʊn] 名 皺眉

split [splɪt] 動 裂開 《into》

wait a moment 等一下

We looked at the piece of paper, open mouthed.

We were in **shock**! But Lolly was very **business-like** and she soon began making plans.

我們看到了那個數字以後，全都張大嘴巴說不出話來。

真是樂翻天的一週。

總共是兩千零九十七萬三千四百五十八元又二十七分英鎊。

我們全嚇呆了！但一板一眼的蘿莉立刻就開始計畫了起來。

shock [ʃɑk] 名 震驚
business-like [ˋbɪznɪs͵laɪk] 形 一板一眼的

獎金金額很龐大。當然我們會提供你們任何有關財務處理方面的建議。如果你們能親自來領取這些獎金，那就再好不過了。

　　但是，我們的鄰居們會怎麼想呢？這樣他們就都知道我們家在玩樂透了！好丟臉啊！

　　你們親自上節目，在公開場合下領獎，這樣是最好不過了。

　　可不可能請狄格來頒發獎金給我們呢？

　　我倒寧願是歌劇明星多‧普拉席德來頒獎呢！

financial [faɪˋnænʃəl] 形 財務的
advice [ədˋvaɪs] 名 意見；忠告
humiliating [hjuˋmɪlɪˏetɪŋ] 形 丟臉的
suppose [səˋpoz] 動 認為；猜測

Lolly got on the phone.

Any chance of getting Dig the pop star, or Dom Placido?

Yes, no problem. We'll get Dig to do the presentation.

How perfectly frightful!

Sorry, Dom Placido was busy.

WOW!

That was it. **There was no way** we'd ever get Clarissa to change her mind. It's **amazing** what money can buy.

蘿莉打了一通電話。

有沒有可能邀請狄格或是多‧普拉席德來當特別來賓呢?

沒問題,狄格可以擔任特別來賓。

太棒了!酷斃了!

抱歉,多‧普拉席德太忙了。

就這樣了。沒有任何人可以改變克萊里莎的心意,金錢果真是萬能的。

presentation [ˌprɛzn̩ˋteʃən] 名 授獎
frightful [ˋfraɪtfəl] 形 非常的;駭人的
there's no way (that) 決不
amazing [əˋmezɪŋ] 形 令人驚異的

The week went by and Saturday finally came. A huge **stretch limo** came to take us to the TV **studios**. It was great. It had a **satellite** TV and video games, a drinks cupboard, phone and a fax. The driver even had a **uniform** with a hat.

You could **tell** the neighbors were well **impressed**.

They won't be talking to the likes of us now.

Oh no!

第五章　上電視

　　一個星期過去，終於到了星期六。一部加長型的禮車特地前來接我們到電視臺的攝影棚。真是太帥了。車上不但有衛星電視、電動遊戲、吧臺、電話和傳真機，連司機叔叔都穿著制服戴著帽子呢！

　　你可以想像我們的鄰居有多麼驚訝。

　　他們這家人現在可不會跟我們這些人打交道了。

　　噢，不！

stretch [strɛtʃ] 形 加長型的

limo [`lɪmo] 名 大型轎車

studio [`stjudɪˏo] 名 攝影棚

satellite [`sætlˏaɪt] 名 衛星

uniform [`junəˏfɔrm] 名 制服

tell [tɛl] 動 明白，知道（通常用 can tell...）

impress [ɪm`prɛs] 動 使留下深刻印象

At the TV station we met Edwin Rich, the
Lottery show **presenter**,

And Mystic Maggie,

The producer showed us where to stand
when we were called on **stage** and then she
showed us to our seats.

到了電視臺後我們見到了樂透開獎的主持人艾德溫・瑞奇。

還有神秘的瑪姬。

嗨！真高興能見到你們！

你們一家人正是我所預見的樣子。

製作人先告訴我們上了舞臺時要站在什麼地方，然後帶我們到座位上去。

presenter [prɪˋzɛntɚ] 名 節目主持人

stage [stedʒ] 名 舞臺

A man started telling jokes to get us all in **a good mood**. Then it was time for the show to begin. We waited nervously in our seats as the producer began to **count down** the seconds.

10 9 8 7 6 5 4 3 2 1

Suddenly the Lottery theme was **blaring** out and the show was live on air.

A tiny village in Cornwall received some money for a new arts center and a tin whistle band played a tune before they got their check to buy new instruments. Then it was our turn. The drums began to roll.

Thrum-drum-diddle-drum-drum-

Last week was a roll-over week and there was only one winning ticket. Here to collect their check for £20,973,458-27p is... the Jackson-Jones family!

有個人先說了一些笑話逗我們開心。然後節目開始的時間到了。當製作人開始倒數計秒的時候，坐在椅子上等待的我們緊張了起來。

10 9 8 7 6 5 4 3 2 1

樂透開獎節目的片頭曲響了起來，現場直播的節目開始了。

康維爾的一個小村莊收下給新藝術中心的捐款，在他們領取添購新樂器的支票之前，他們的錫笛樂團還演奏了一段樂曲。然後就輪到我們了，鼓聲開始響了起來。

咚—咚—咚—咚—咚—

上個星期果真是樂翻天的一週，得獎人只有一個。獎金金額高達兩千零九十七萬三千四百五十八元又二十七分英鎊。現在讓我們歡迎得獎人……傑克森—瓊斯家族！

mood [mud] 名 心情
a good mood 好心情
count [kaʊnt] 動 數
count down 倒數計秒
blare [blɛr] 動 播放；響起 《out》

We were blinded by the lights that were **focused** on our seats. We **staggered** up to the stage and stood on our marks. We were all **grinning** like idiots! Mum pretended it was all a big surprise.

We've never bought a ticket before, you know. We thought we'd try it once, for a laugh!

Then a screen behind us **ripped** in two and there stood Dig! Clarissa fainted.

Hi!

WOOSH

FAINT

突來的一道強光打在我們的座位上，照得我們睜不開眼。我們顫抖地走上舞臺，站在已事先作了記號的位置上。每個人咧著嘴笑得像個傻瓜一樣！媽媽還裝出一副欣喜若狂的表情。

你們知道嗎？我們家從沒買過樂透券。我們不過是覺得應該嘗試一次，好玩嘛！

接著我們身後的屏風裂成兩半，是狄格，他就站在那邊！克萊里莎一看到他就昏倒了。

嗨！

focus [ˋfokəs] 勔 集中 《on》
stagger [ˋstægɚ] 勔 步履不穩地走
grin [grɪn] 勔 露齒微笑
rip [rɪp] 勔 破裂

There's not a lot you can do when someone gives you so much money.

We carried on grinning until it **hurt**.

By the time Clarissa **came round** Dig was long gone.

我很榮幸能將這份非常非常貴重的支票頒給你們。現在就把它打開，你們一定會非常開心的。

　　這個年輕人真和善。

　　當有人送了這麼大一筆金錢給你的時候，其實真的不曉得說什麼才好。

　　所以，我們只好繼續微笑直到下巴開始酸痛。

　　而當克萊里莎醒過來的時候，狄格早就已經離去多時了。

　　噢，媽咪！我根本沒來得及親他一下。把狄格買下來給我好不好，拜……託啦！

present [prɪ`zɛnt] 動 贈送

hurt [hɝt] 動 弄痛

come round 甦醒，恢復知覺

$\mathcal{W}$e all slept late the next morning. The first **inkling** of what was to come came on the radio as Dad was shaving in the bathroom.

...The giant Lottery win couldn't have come at a better time for the father of the Jackson-Jones Family who, it is rumored, was to lose his job next week...

What?

Later that morning, Mum was watching television in the kitchen when **suddenly**, her best friend appeared on the screen.

第六章　不敢相信

　　第二天我們都睡得很晚。事情是從爸爸在浴室裡一邊刮鬍子，一邊聽著收音機的時候開始的。

　　巨額樂透彩金對於傑克森─瓊斯家的男主人來說並不是一件好事，因為謠傳這位父親在下星期就要失業了……

　　什麼？

　　稍晚一點，媽媽在廚房裡看電視，突然，她看到了她最好的朋友出現在螢幕上。

inkling [`ɪŋklɪŋ] 名 暗示；透露
rumor [`rumɚ] 動 謠傳（用 be rumored）
suddenly [`sʌdn̩lɪ] 副 突然地

And when I **switched on** the lunchtime news program there was my teacher.

As for Clarissa, she heard something rather unpleasant on her headphones.

我已經認識她很多年了，她可以說是個非常自大傲慢的人，但是啊，你怎麼想得到她會……

什麼！

我把電視轉到午間新聞的時候，我的導師居然出現在節目裡。

你不能說約翰是世界上最聰明的學生。事實上，他一點也稱不上……

什麼！

至於克萊里莎，則從耳機裡聽到更不愉快的消息。

狄格說那個樂透獎得主家裡的那個頭髮有瀏海的女兒，看起來跟個笨蛋沒兩樣！

什麼！

snooty [`snutɪ] 形 高傲自大的
switch [swɪtʃ] 動 開（關）
switch on 打開
switch off 關掉

We went to get the Sunday papers, to **cheer** ourselves **up**. It was a huge mistake. We were on the front page of every one. Almost anyone we had ever spoken to had sold their stories.

ENQUIRER

SHOCK HORROR

Snobby Mum

Sunday Rock

Lottery-winning daughter is stupid, pop music crazy has a head full of pink cotton wool and terrible spots says her frien

SUNDAY VACUUM

all the dirt and lots of sucking-up!

Useless Lottery-winning father had fourteen girlfriends before he got married. They say what they think of him inside.

Young Sunday

Thicko Lottery-winning son is no good at school, cheats at games, girls fancy hi

我們跑去買了星期天的報紙，希望看了以後可以高興一些。可是呢，真是大錯特錯。每一份報紙的頭版都是我們，幾乎每個曾和我們講過話的人都發表了一篇故事。

　　《調查者》真令人不敢相信，傲慢的母親……

　　《星期天搖滾》對於樂透獎得主的女兒，朋友說她是一個笨蛋，瘋狂的迷戀流行音樂，頭髮上永遠都掛著粉紅色羊毛彩帶，還長滿著雀斑。

　　《真空星期天》沒用的人，贏得樂透獎的這個爸爸在結婚以前共交過１４個女朋友。她們說出了對他的評價……

　　《年輕星期天》樂透獎得主的兒子在學校裡一點也不優秀，玩遊戲的時候都會作弊；學校裡的女孩們根本就不想理他。

cheer up　激勵

Enquirer [ɪnˋkwaɪrɚ]　名 詢問者；調查者

騙……人！

他們怎麼能這麼說呢！

呃……這好像是真的！

天啊，真丟臉，我怎麼面對其他人啊！在這一切平息下來以前，我們一定要先離開這裡。

blow [blo] 勳 吹散；吹

blow over 過去

CHAPTER SEVEN
Getaway

_L_uckily, when you're rich you can do almost anything you like whenever you want to.

So, on Monday morning we went down to the travel **agents**.

第七章　逃離

　　幸運的是，當你有錢的時候，你幾乎可以在任何時候做你想做的任何事情。

　　所以，在星期一一早我們就來到了旅行社。

　　我們想要儘快離開這裡，到陽光明媚、海水湛藍又溫暖的地方。

　　我查一下電腦……對了，就是這裡，明天早上你們就可以在天堂般的地方吃早餐了。

　　聽起來好棒。

getaway [`gɛtəˌwe] 名 逃亡，逃走
agent [`edʒənt] 名 經紀人；代理人
breakfast [`brɛkfəst] 動 吃早餐
paradise [`pærəˌdaɪs] 名 樂園；天堂

We **rushed** home, **packed** a few things, and phoned for a taxi to take us to the airport. Soon we were flying in a beautiful blue sky.

Before long we were **settling** into our sun-**drenched** tropical island total vacation location. We thought we were in paradise.

我們衝回家，打包了簡單的行李，然後叫了一部計程車載我們到機場。很快的，我們就飛翔在美麗的藍天之上了。

　　啊哈！這就是人生！

　　沒多久我們便到了渡假聖地，我們那灑滿陽光的熱帶島嶼。我們以為是到了天堂。

rush [rʌʃ] 動 直奔
pack [pæk] 動 打包
settle [`sɛtḷ] 動（飛機）降落；安身
drench [drɛntʃ] 動 使溼透

We weren't. We had the worst holiday you can imagine.

We **suffered** from **sunburn**

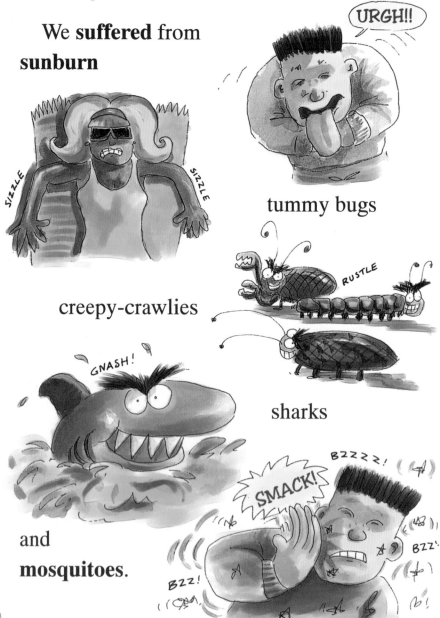

tummy bugs

creepy-crawlies

sharks

and **mosquitoes**.

錯了，我們的假期糟透了。
我們不僅曬傷了
肚子痛
到處是毛毛蟲
鯊魚
和蚊子。

suffer [`sʌfɚ] 動 痛苦 《from》
sunburn [`sʌn͵bɝn] 名 曬傷
mosquito [mə`skito] 名 蚊子

Worse still, someone recognized us from the papers...

...and soon Clarissa had loads of **admirers** who had found out how rich we were.

Dad spent all his time chasing them off.

On the way home, the plane was **delayed** for sixteen hours and we had to fly through a tropical storm. We looked pretty **rough** when we landed.

更糟糕的是，有人看過報紙，認出了我們……

你不就是那個樂透獎的得主嗎？

嗯……對的。

你真漂亮！

……很快的，克萊里莎的身後就跟了一堆知道我們有多富有的仰慕者。

爸爸全部的時間都用來趕走他們。

在回家的路上，飛機延遲了十六個小時，而且在途中我們還遭遇了熱帶風暴。當飛機降落的時候，我們每個人看起來都非常狼狽。

我想吐！

admirer [əd`maɪrɚ] 名 仰慕者

delay [dɪ`le] 動 延期

rough [rʌf] 形 身體不舒服的；難受的

sick [sɪk] 形 噁心的；反胃的

CHAPTER EIGHT
Welcome Home

$\mathcal{W}$e were really pleased to be back. It was cold, it was raining and there wasn't a shark in sight.

But when we got home, we could hardly get through the front door. The **hallway** was full of mail, and 99.9% of it was **begging** letters.

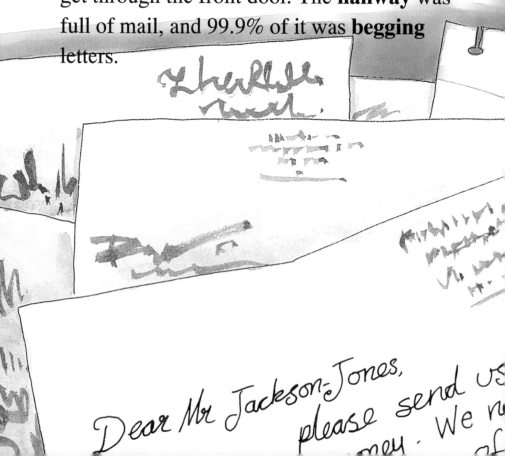

Dear Mr Jackson-Jones, please send us ... money. We n...

Dear Jackson-Jones Family,
Congratulations on your fabulou[s]
Lottery Jackpot win.
In your hour of success, may [I]
I draw your attention to our lit[tle]
charity that looks aft[er]
sick mic[e]

16

10 m
Mar

Dear Clarissa,
have you ever thought about
all those poor rock-music[ians]
who need money to
more musi[c]
Pl[ease]

第八章 歡迎回家

我們真的很高興回家。天氣雖然很冷，還下著雨，但是看不到鯊魚。

可是當我們一到達家門口的時候，幾乎沒辦法從大門口走進去。整條走廊都是郵件，而且百分之九十九點九都是要求捐款的信件。

親愛的傑克森－瓊斯太太，

請寄些錢給我們，我們急需要錢。謝謝。

hallway [ˋhɔl͵we] 名 走廊

beg [bɛg] 動 乞求

親愛的傑克森─瓊斯家庭，

恭賀閣下一家榮獲樂透大獎之殊榮。在您享受成功之際，容我將閣下的注意力轉移至可憐的病老鼠身上……

親愛的克萊里莎，

你有沒有想過我們這些貧窮的，需要金錢支援來創造更好音樂的搖滾音樂家？

congratulation [kən‚grætʃə`leʃən] 名 恭喜
（通常用 congratulations）
fabulous [`fæbjələs] 形 令人難以置信的
draw [drɔ] 動 吸引，引起

We got quite **depressed** reading all those letters. Most of them went in the bin, but there must have been at least three hundred that were really **worthy** causes. We put them in a box and promised to **deal with** them later.

What we needed was some advice. We telephoned Lolly Priceworth and she put us in touch with Mr Smiley, who was a financial **adviser**.

在看完這些信件以後，我們變得相當沮喪。雖然大部分都進了垃圾桶，但是至少有三百封是理由相當充分的。我們將那些信件收在一個盒子裡，並決定稍後再來處理它們。

當前我們最需要的是一些建議。我們打電話給蘿莉・普萊斯渥斯，然後她介紹史麥立先生給我們，他是一位財務金融專家。

depress [dɪ`prɛs] 動 使沮喪
worthy [`wɝðɪ] 形 值得的
deal with 處理
adviser [əd`vaɪzɚ] 名 顧問

You are exceedingly rich. You would be better off moving to a larger house, away from nosy neighbors.

你們現在是大富翁了。最好是搬到大一點的房子，離開這些好管閒事的鄰居。

exceedingly [ɪk`sidɪŋlɪ] 副 非常地；極度地

away from... 離開…

nosy [`nozɪ] 形 好管閒事的

We took his advice, and after days trailing around huge mansions, we bought one of them, and Dad bought several large cars so that we could travel there in style.

It was the house of all our dreams.

I got a motorbike to ride around on and a soundproof room of my own with a mega-loud CD system and disco lights!

我們接受了他的意見，在找了幾天的豪宅之後，我們買下了其中的一棟。爸爸也買了好幾部大車子以便符合我們現在高尚的生活。

　　這是一幢集合我們所有夢想的房子。

車　庫

三溫暖

游泳池

建身房

網球場

馬 房

撳浴缸

槌球場

　　我有一部摩托車可以騎來騎去；在我的房間裡不但有如迪斯可一樣炫麗的燈光，還裝了隔音設備，可以儘情享受我那超大瓦數的ＣＤ音響。

RRRM!

CHAPTER NINE
School

Now that we had a big, posh house and drove around in big, posh cars, Mum said I couldn't possibly go back to my **nasty** old school, not after what my teacher had said about me. So I was packed off to St Toff's **boarding school**.

第九章　新學校

　　現在我們家是又大又豪華，開的也是又大又氣派的車子，所以媽媽說我不能再回到以前那間又老又討厭的學校，更何況是我的導師把我說成那個樣子。所以我就轉學到聖多福住宿學校去了。

　　真不敢相信這就是制服！

nasty [`næstɪ] 形 令人討厭的
boarding [`bɔrdɪŋ] 名 寄宿
boarding school 寄宿學校

All the boys there had noses that stuck up in the air as though there was a bad smell in the place.

All their mums and dads were either Lords or Ladies, Sirs or **Right Honorables**.

Of course, since I wasn't **aristocratic**, and our family hadn't stolen all our money from the peasants five hundred years ago, I was **treated** as the school joke.

They gave me all sorts of **nicknames** but as our money came from the Lottery, the name Lotty stuck!

在那邊的男孩子每個人都有一個朝天鼻，好像那裡的空氣很難聞的樣子。

　　他們的父母親不是伯爵或貴婦，就是爵士或貴族。

　　當然，因為我不是貴族，我們的家族也沒有在五百年前偷取農夫們的金錢，所以在學校裡，我便被當成了一個大笑話。

　　因為我們家的財富是來自於樂透獎，所以我所有的綽號都被冠上「樂透」兩個字。

　　幸運的吉姆！

　　樂透球！

　　樂透仔！

the Right Honorable　伯爵
aristocratic [ə,rɪstə`krætɪk] 形 貴族的
treat [trit] 動 當作 《as》
nickname [`nɪk,nem] 名 綽號

The food was terrible...

Urgh!

...we had too much homework...

...and at night, I would lie in my bed in the **dormitory**, unable to get to sleep.

學校的食物真是難吃⋯⋯
⋯⋯還有寫不完的家庭作業⋯⋯
⋯⋯而晚上，躺在宿舍的床上，我根本無法睡著。

dormitory [ˋdɔrməˏtɔrɪ] 名 宿舍

CHAPTER TEN
The Summer Holidays

At last the end of **term** came, and our new **butler** came to **pick** me **up** in a Rolls-Royce.

Let me carry your bags for you, young sir.

第十章 暑假

終於挨到學期結束了，家裡新聘的管家開著勞斯萊斯到學校接我。

少爺，行李讓我來拿就可以了。

term [tɝm] 名 學期
butler [ˋbʌtlɚ] 名 管家
pick up 用車去接（人）

As **well as** a butler, Mum and Dad had got a cook. The food she made was **awful**, but I was not **allowed** to say so.

She couldn't even make chips!

The cook and the butler were so snooty, they made Mum feel like **dirt**. When she asked them to do something they would say things like:

But Madam, we never did it like that when we were with Lord So & So.

Ah!

除了管家以外，爸媽也聘了一位廚師來料理我們的伙食。她所煮出來的食物真是難吃到了極點，但是我又不能說出來。她甚至不會做洋芋片。

廚師和管家是如此的目中無人，根本沒有將媽媽看在眼裡。每當媽媽要求他們做些不一樣的菜，就會聽到如下的回答：

不行啊，夫人，我們在伯爵家工作的時候，根本就沒做過那些菜。

as well as 除…之外還…

awful [`ɔful] 形 極糟的

allow [ə`lau] 動 允許

dirt [dɝt] 名 灰塵；垃圾

treat someone like dirt 對（人）完全缺乏尊重

Mum **took their word for it**. She spent all her time **tidying** and cleaning and cooking and doing all the jobs that she wanted doing, while the cook and the butler sat around enjoying themselves!

My old friend Kevin came to stay for a few days but we didn't **get on**. He said that money had changed me.

而媽媽也信以為真，所以當管家和廚師坐在椅子上享受的時候，媽媽自己整天就做著打掃、清潔、做菜還有其他她自己想做的工作。

　　我的好友凱文來我們家住了幾天，可是我們並沒有處得很好。他說金錢已經改變了我。

　　我沒有變，是我身邊的事物改變了。

　　可憐的有錢小孩！

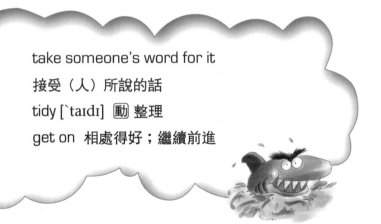

take someone's word for it
接受（人）所說的話
tidy [`taɪdɪ] 動 整理
get on 相處得好；繼續前進

During the summer holidays, we had a huge party for all our friends. But **instead of** being one big party, it ended up as four different parties. There were Mum and Dad's new rich friends in one corner...

...our old friends in another...

在暑假的時候，我們邀請了我們所有的朋友來家裡參加派對。但是，整個派對並沒有如我們所想的是一個超大型的聚會，到後來，成了四個小團體。角落裡是媽媽和爸爸有錢的新朋友……

金錢並不代表一切。

鬼屋喲。

……我們的老朋友在另一邊……

對我們來說太奢華了。

多美好的房子。

instead of 代替

...our relations **huddled** in the kitchen, **moaning** about how mean we were with our money...

> They only gave our Tracy £10 for her Birthday!

...and Clarissa, who was having boyfriend trouble, dancing by herself to Dig's CDs...

> Men! They only want me for my money. They don't want me for myself. No one understands that I'm a deeply emotional person.

……我們的親戚聚集在廚房裡，抱怨著我們有多吝嗇……

我們家崔西過生日時，他們竟然只給了她１０鎊！

……克萊里莎呢，因為和男朋友吵架，所以一個人跟著狄格的音樂跳舞……

臭男人！只想要我的錢，根本不是喜歡我的人。根本沒有人知道我是個感情非常脆弱的人。

huddle [ˋhʌdl̩] 動 聚集在一起

moan [mon] 動 發牢騷

emotional [ɪˋmoʃən̩l] 形 感情脆弱的；易感的

It was a **disaster**. Our relatives started
arguing about money and it wasn't long
before the party **ended up** in a fight.

Mum and Dad's new friends walked out in
disgust. So did the cook and butler.

The party was over in more ways than one. Money had only brought us unhappiness. We became lazy and forgot to **tidy up** and empty the bins. The place **went to rack and ruin**. So did Mum and Dad.

災難開始了，親戚們開始為了錢起爭執，過沒多久，竟然打了起來，當然派對也就這麼草草結束了。

　　淘金者！

　　小氣鬼！

　　暴發戶！

　　爸媽的新朋友一臉厭惡地離去，連管家和廚師也是。

　　我們從來沒看過這麼低級又下流的行為！

　　我們也是。

disaster [dɪz`æstɚ] 名 災難

argue [`ɑrgjʊ] 動 爭論

end up 以…告終 《in》

disgust [dɪs`gʌst] 名 厭惡

這場派對的結局並非只有一種。金錢竟然只帶給我們不快樂。我們變成懶人，沒有打掃房子，也沒有倒垃圾，整個屋子零亂不堪，爸爸媽媽連動也不想動一下。

再送一客披薩來！

tidy up 整理
rack [ræk] 名 荒廢；破壞
ruin [`ruɪn] 名 荒廢；沒落
go to rack and ruin 荒廢

A while after the party, I was **rooting** around in the back of a cupboard, hoping to find something clean to wear, when I **came across** a cardboard box.

Inside were the begging letters that we received after our Lottery win. I started to read them. I was still there half an hour later when Dad found me.

> What've you got there, Son?

第十一章 終於明白

　　派對過後幾天，我翻箱倒櫃，想找一件乾淨的衣服來換，就在那個時候我看到了一個小盒子。

　　裡頭裝的就是我們在贏得樂透獎以後，收到的那些請求援助的信件。我開始一封一封讀了起來，當爸爸在半小時以後找到我時，我還在那裡。

　　兒子，你找到了什麼？

root [rut] 動 翻找東西 《around》
come across 偶然發現；遇見

103

He read some of the letters.

We showed the letters to Mum and Clarissa. It didn't take long before we all **came to our senses**.

We had a family **pow-wow** and decided what we were going to do. We spent the rest of the day answering all the letters in the box and putting £1,000 checks in each of the **envelopes**.

爸爸也讀了其中幾封信。

這些人的遭遇真的好可憐。

我們現在也是呀，爸爸。

我們把那些信件拿給媽媽和克萊里莎看，沒多久，我們的腦筋全都恢復了理性。

金錢真的沒有帶給我們任何的快樂，對不對？

我們開了個家庭會議決定應該怎麼做。我們開始回覆盒子裡的每一封信，還在每個信封裡面附上英鎊一千元的支票。

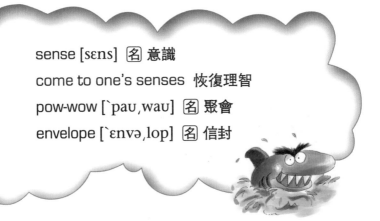

sense [sɛns] 名 意識

come to one's senses 恢復理智

pow-wow [`pau,wau] 名 聚會

envelope [`ɛnvə,lop] 名 信封

Then we sold the house...

...and the cars.

(Well, Dad was allowed to keep the Jag!)

And we bought our old house back.

然後我們把大房子賣掉⋯⋯

⋯⋯還有車子。

（不過呢，爸爸被允許保留一部捷豹的車子！）

接著，我們將原來的房子買回來。

開價吧。

要多少錢？

We made sure that everyone was paid off and that we didn't **owe** anybody anything, then we looked at our bank **account**.

Because the money had been earning **interest**, we actually had more money now than we had won **in the first place**!

在確定每一張支票都已經兌現，而且我們沒有虧欠他人任何東西之後，我們去銀行查看戶頭上的餘額。

　　由於存款可以賺取利息，所以，我們現在的存款比剛贏得獎金的時候還要多！

　　現在我們總共有兩千兩百五十萬英鎊！

owe [o] 動 欠債

account [əˋkaʊnt] 名 存款戶頭

interest [ˋɪntərɪst] 名 利息

in the first place　本來；首先

We chose our favorite charities.

Mum gave five and a half million to *Help the Children.*

Dad gave five and a half million to *Help the Old People.*

Clarissa split five and a half million between *Help the Whales* and *Help the Rainforest.*

I gave five and a half million to *Save the Animals.*

每個人選擇了自己最想要捐助的對象。

　　媽媽捐了五百五十萬給「幫助兒童基金會」。

　　爸爸捐了五百五十萬給「幫助老人基金會」。

　　克萊里莎的五百五十萬捐給了「拯救鯨魚協會」和「拯救雨林協會」。

　　我則是將五百五十萬捐給了「動物保護協會」。

That left five hundred thousand pounds.

We went to the bank and **withdrew** the money in **cash**. It **filled** two suitcases.

Then we phoned the TV station and told them to meet us on top of the tallest building in the country: The Universal Trade Tower.

最後還剩下五十萬英鎊。

我們到銀行把剩下的錢全部領出來，鈔票裝了整整兩大箱。

接下來，我們打電話給電視臺，告訴他們到全國最高的建築物——世界貿易中心——來找我們。

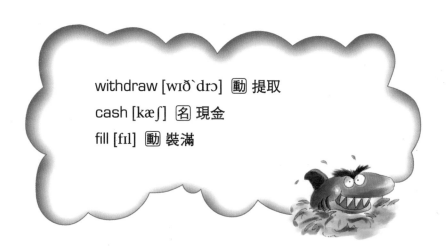

withdraw [wɪðˋdrɔ] 動 提取

cash [kæʃ] 名 現金

fill [fɪl] 動 裝滿

We waited until the **cameras** were rolling,
then we threw the money to **the four winds**.

There were cameras on the ground too.
That night, on the TV news, we watched
how the people down below had **scrabbled**
and fought as the money came **floating** down
from the sky.

I hope we made someone happy.

等到攝影機開拍以後，我們就將錢從四面八方灑了下去。

地面上也有攝影機。當天晚上的電視新聞，我們看到人們是如何拼命爭奪這些從天而降的鈔票。

我希望有人因此快樂起來。

camera [`kæmərə] 名 電視攝影機

wind [wɪnd] 名 風

the four winds 四面八方；東西南北風

scrabble [`skræbl̩] 動 抓

float [flot] 動 飄動；漂浮

CHAPTER TWELVE
A Happy Ending

Mum's happy now. She doesn't feel she has to be posh any more.

Dad's still got his Jag which is all he ever really wanted.

第十二章 皆大歡喜

　　媽媽現在很快樂，她不再覺得自己需要裝得雍容華貴。

　　我已經經歷過那樣的日子了。

　　而爸爸則保留了他夢寐以求的捷豹汽車。

　　我的驕傲與快樂！

And I'm back at my old school and best **mates** with Kevin again, like nothing had ever happened.

But Clarissa is the really happy one. She's got a new boyfriend who, she says, looks just like Dig. And she says he really loves her for herself.

He must do...who else would have her without a couple of million **thrown in**?!

我又回到原來的學校，再度和凱文成為最佳拍檔，就好像事情從來沒有發生過一樣。

克萊里莎應該是最快樂的人了。她交了一個新男朋友，根據她的說法，這個人長得跟狄格很像，而且他是真的因為喜歡她這個人才跟她交往的。

他一定是喜歡她的……沒了幾百萬鈔票當嫁妝，還有誰會喜歡她呢？！

啊，他真好！

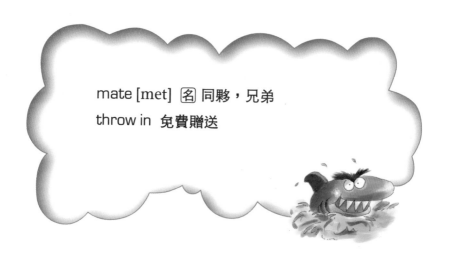

mate [met] 名 同夥，兄弟

throw in 免費贈送

SAVOIR PLUS

專為十歲以上青少年設計的百科全書

人類文明小百科

行政院新聞局第十六次推介中小學生優良課外讀物

(1)歐洲的城堡
(2)法老時代的埃及
(3)羅馬人
(4)希臘人
(5)希伯來人
(6)高盧人
(7)樂器
(8)史前人類
(9)火山與地震

(10)探索與發現
(11)從行星到眾星系
(12)電影
(13)科學簡史
(14)奧林匹克運動會
(15)音樂史
(16)身體與健康
(17)神話

全套一共17冊／每冊定價250元

讓您的孩子發現文明，擁有世界

超級科學家系列
SUPER SCIENTISTS

中英對照，既可學英語又可了解偉人小故事哦！

當彗星掠過哈雷眼前，

當蘋果落在牛頓頭項，

當電燈泡在愛迪生手中亮起⋯⋯

一個個求知的心靈與真理所碰撞出的火花，

那就是《超級科學家系列》！

神祕元素：居禮夫人的故事　含CD190元

望遠天際：伽利略的故事　含CD190元

爆炸性的發現：諾貝爾的故事　含CD190元

宇宙教授：愛因斯坦的故事　含CD190元

電燈的發明：愛迪生的故事　含CD190元

光的顏色：牛頓的故事　定價160元

蠶寶寶的祕密：巴斯德的故事　含CD190元

命運的彗星：哈雷的故事　含CD190元

自然英語系列

自然英語系列

你將會發現：學英語竟然可以這麼自自然然、輕輕鬆鬆！

自然英語會話

大西泰斗著／Paul C. McVay 著

用生動、簡單易懂的筆調，針對口語的特殊動詞表現、日常生活的口頭禪等方面，解說生活英語精髓，使你的英語會話更接近以英語為母語的人，更流利、更自然。

英文自然學習法（一）

大西泰斗著／Paul C. McVay 著

針對被動語態、時態、進行式與完成式、Wh-疑問句與關係詞等重點分析解說，讓你輕鬆掌握英文文法的竅門。

英文自然學習法（二）

大西泰斗著／Paul C. McVay 著

打破死背介系詞意義和片語的方式，將介系詞的各種衍生用法連繫起來，讓你自然掌握介系詞的感覺和精神。

英文自然學習法（三）

大西泰斗著／Paul C. McVay 著

運用「兔子和鴨子」的原理，解說PRESSURE的MUST、POWER的WILL、UP／DOWN／OUT／OFF等用法的基本感覺，以及所衍生出各式各樣精采豐富的意思，讓你簡單輕鬆活用英語！

國家圖書館出版品預行編目資料

我家中樂透／Shoo Rayner 著；刊欣媒體營造工作室
譯－－初版. －－臺北市：三民，民89
　　面；　公分
中英對照
ISBN 957–14–3266–0（平裝）

1.英國語言－讀本

805.18　　　　　　　　　　　　　89010074

網際網路位址　http://www. sanmin. com. tw

ⓒ 我家中樂透

作者兼
繪圖者　Damon Burnard
譯　者　刊欣媒體營造工作室
發行人　劉振強
著作財
產權人　三民書局股份有限公司
　　　　臺北市復興北路三八六號
發行所　三民書局股份有限公司
　　　　地址／臺北市復興北路三八六號
　　　　電話／二五○○六六○○
　　　　郵撥／○○○九九九八——五號
印刷所　三民書局股份有限公司
門市部　復北店／臺北市復興北路三八六號
　　　　重南店／臺北市重慶南路一段六十一號
初版一刷　中華民國八十九年十月
編　號　S85506
定　價　新臺幣貳佰陸拾元整

行政院新聞局登記證局版臺業字第○二○○號

有著作權　不准侵害

ISBN　957–14–3266–0（平裝）